Hello, Family Members,

Learning to read is one of the most important accomplishments of early childhood. **Hello Reader!** books are designed to help children become skilled readers who like to read. Beginning readers learn to read by remembering frequently used words like "the," "is," and "and"; by using phonics skills to decode new words; and by interpreting picture and text clues. These books provide both the stories children enjoy and the structure they need to read fluently and independently. Here are suggestions for helping your child *before*, *during*, and *after* reading:

Before

- Look at the cover and pictures and have your child predict what the story is about.
- Read the story to your child.
- Encourage your child to chime in with familiar words and phrases.
- Echo read with your child by reading a line first and having your child read it after you do.

During

- Have your child think about a word he or she does not recognize right away. Provide hints such as "Let's see if we know the sounds" and "Have we read other words like this one?"
- Encourage your child to use phonics skills to sound out new words.
- Provide the word for your child when more assistance is needed so that he or she does not struggle and the experience of reading with you is a positive one.
- Encourage your child to have fun by reading with a lot of expression . . . like an actor!

After

- Have your child keep lists of interesting and favorite words.
- Encourage your child to read the books over and over again. Have him or her read to brothers, sisters, grandparents, and even teddy bears. Repeated readings develop confidence in young readers.
- Talk about the stories. Ask and answer questions. Share ideas about the funniest and most interesting characters and events in the stories.

I do hope that you and your child enjoy this book.

—Francie Alexander
Reading Specialist,
Scholastic's Learning Ventur

D1110398

For Nina and all my dear dogs.
—F.M.

My love and thanks to
Rob and Nell for their contributions.
—J.D.

Text copyright © 1999 by Faith McNulty.
Illustrations copyright © 1999 by Julie Durrell.
All rights reserved. Published by Scholastic Inc.
SCHOLASTIC, HELLO READER, CARTWHEEL BOOKS
and associated logos are trademarks and/or
registered trademarks of Scholastic Inc.

Library of Congress Cataloging-in-Publication Data

Faith McNulty.
    If dogs ruled the world / by Faith McNulty; illustrated by Julie Durrell.
        p.   cm. — (Hello reader! Level 3)
    Summary: In a world where dogs ruled, people would be well treated
as pets.
    ISBN 0-439-08752-X
    [1. Dogs fiction.   2. Pets Fiction.]   I. Durrell, Julie, ill.
    II. Title.   III. Series.
PZ7.M478815If 1999
[E]—dc21   99-24785
                                                               CIP
12 11 10 9 8 7 6 5 4 3 2   9/9 0/0 01 02 03 04

Printed in the U.S.A.
First printing, September 1999

If Dogs Ruled The World

by Faith McNulty
Illustrated by Julie Durrell

Hello Reader!— Level 3

SCHOLASTIC INC.
Cartwheel ·B·O·O·K·S·®

New York   Toronto   London   Auckland   Sydney
Mexico City   New Delhi   Hong Kong

If dogs ruled the world,
they would keep people as pets.

They would keep them in a fenced yard
so that they couldn't run away.

Some people would be house people
and go out for walks on a leash.

Lucky people would live on a farm
and be free to run,
but mostly they would want to stay
near their dog.

Kind dogs would take good care of
their people.
They would take them to the vet
for shots and checkups.
The vet might say, "No more bones for
this person. Try dry food."

A dog might take his person to a
pet store that had people toys—
dolls and trucks, roller skates
and baseball bats.
The dog might buy his person a fancy
collar with its name on a tag,
in case the person got lost.

The dog might buy a box of
people biscuits or a special
people treat, like cookies and
doughnuts or lollipops,
and a dinner plate with
PERSON written on it.

A dog might buy a brush just for
grooming people and flea powder
and a person shampoo.

But some dogs would wash
their person the old-fashioned way,
by licking it clean.

Dogs love puppies.
If a dog family had puppies,
it would get them a baby
to play with.

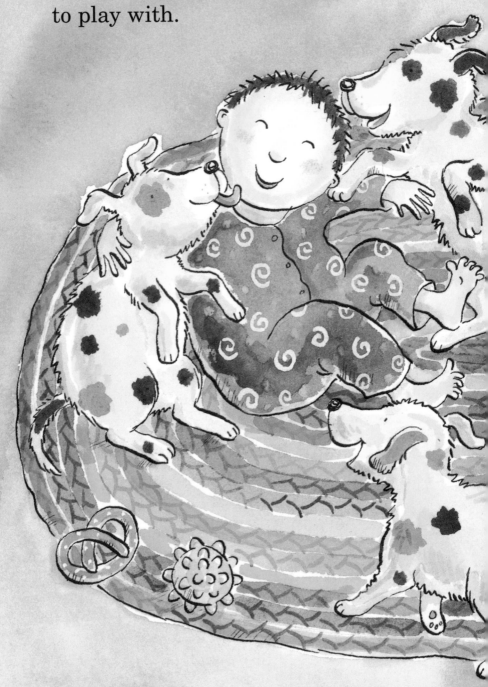

They would show the puppies
how to hold the baby nicely
and carry it in their teeth
without hurting it.

When the baby grew older,
its dogs would show it how to chase
a ball and play catch.

Dogs would read books on training children to sit and lie down.

The reward would be a furry hug
and a loving dog kiss.

Older people would be trained
to guard their house
and let their dogs know when
a strange dog came into the yard.

Good people owners would love their
people very much.
They would take them everywhere—
rides in the car,

walks in the woods,

picnics on the beach.

Good dogs would pet their people a lot.
At night, they would let their person
curl up right next to them in bed
and sleep warm and cozy
surrounded by fur.

It seems too bad that dogs
don't rule the world.